Biography of Deception

by Maria Glymph

A Modern Odyssey Book

For Tom
...bigger than Texas

Snow

Snow cascaded in a soft opaque haze. The arms of the conference room clock slid into place and saluted the tenth hour. A moment prior, the table had been littered with belongings, but they were quickly being gathered as everyone shuffled out into the corridor and back toward their desks. The chill of winter had seeped into the crevices of the meeting, and the outgoing mood was cool and biting.

She lingered momentarily with a thought, shrugged, and approached her seat to pick up her things. The phone and computer sat alone. She looked around and underneath the table. "It's gone." With a whisper, she realized that her fortress had been breached, and then fear handed her a cloak of panic.

Her notebook was missing.

HUDDLE

Sloane didn't want to be outraged. It was too early in the morning, and it was Monday. There would be plenty of time for displeasure later in the week when she provided performance feedback to her team and committed cuts to her boss. This just wasn't the moment to allow visceral emotions to surface.

Yet, she could not suppress a low groan, rumbling and rising as if a wave were building toward the shore, preparing to crash onto the sand and drag everything it could grab as it receded into the sea.

She closed her eyes and drew in a deep breath.

They're an opportunistic bunch, she thought, and an urgent curiosity made her wonder where the notebook could be. She smiled. It was wry, more of a smirk. *Who has it and why haven't they returned it?* She was right to be intrigued. Surely whoever had picked it up would have noticed that it was not their own. While Sloane didn't feel anything nefarious had transpired, she speculated as to why her notebook had not yet been brought forward. She disliked conjecture, and yet here she was, faced with an unfortunate and potentially damning situation. And so, suspicion rose and encircled her like a cloud of gnats.

Amelia glanced around. They stood in the small meeting room where they often spoke to have privacy. The glass walls were lightly frosted but not opaque, and Amelia could see into the hallway and out of the building through the glass-paneled walls. Snow fell. Amelia was both puzzled and empathetic. "I've looked in the conference room again," she said, turning to Sloane and fanning a post-it pad as if it were a deck of cards. "I'll go ask everyone to check their things, and then I'll take a look in the common areas in case it somehow ended up there." She understood what was at stake and could already feel the echo of consequence. In the little more than six months that she had been Sloane's assistant, Amelia had discreetly observed as Sloane erupted with rage at a delivery clerk or quietly seethed at her own boss for delivering a presentation to the CEO without her. This was different. Amelia sensed an undercurrent of fear. *But fear of what?*

"What else would you like me to do?" She asked. "The obvious," Sloane said, as she looked up and her gaze cut sharply across the room. "Find it." Their eyes remained locked for what seemed to Amelia like a full minute, and then Sloane enunciated her words, "I want to know who has it — and what they've done with it. I want to know if they looked inside. What they saw. What they read. I want to see how they react when they hand it over — and understand why it took them so long."

Sloane turned toward the door to leave. "To be perfectly transparent Amelia, my notebook contains many things, including confidential company information. But more importantly, it contains my thoughts and reflections. Sometimes they are about people on this team, and as you know, I don't mince words." Her eyes blazed. "My notebook is not for public consumption."

Sloane had shifted from agitation to alarm to disquiet, and she was now on the cusp of rage. The air around her sizzled, Amelia thought that should Sloane step outside, she'd melt the snow.

"I understand," Amelia said, nodding her head. She was familiar with the tone, the stiffening of the back, and the invisible grinding of the heels into the ground. "I'll text you or come find you." Sloane marched out of the room and down the grey corridor. Amelia's voice trailed in her wake.

OUT IN THE OPEN

Amelia felt as if she were walking into a snow globe as she rounded the corner to the open space area and looked out of the floor-to-ceiling windows. The snow continued to swirl and fall, and there was much activity as if someone had shaken their little dome. The world was shut out. Or perhaps they were being contained, kept from the world. The snow cascaded around them, a gauze barrier.

She disliked this space and office spaces in general. They were uninteresting. Gray, drab, boring. There was a psychology behind the neutrality of the setting and the desire to minimize fatigue that could come from overstimulation. Caused by what? In a word: color. Instead — charcoal, steel, stone, graphite. Beautiful words. Dull in this reality. *But how real was it anyway?*

"Okay listen up everyone." She looked across the top of the cubicles. Some people were preparing to head off to meetings. Others were seated. Bodies shifted back and forth. "Monday is not off to a good start." Her voice trembled.

Heads turned toward her. Bodies rose from their seats. Those who had been walking away from the area paused and turned around. "When we left our meeting earlier, someone picked up Sloane's notebook. Easy to have a mix up with company issued supplies." Amelia projected her voice. "Sloane wants it back without delay." She made eye contact as she glanced around the room. "You know how she is when she wants something." She nodded her head for confirmation. "And you know how she is when she doesn't get it." Amelia paused for effect. "I need that notebook. So would you please look and see if you have it."

The tempo changed in an instant, and a dense commotion ensued. Heads bobbed up and down as hands shuffled folders, notebooks, and other items piled on desks. Mouths silently said 'no.' Heads shook back and forth. Shoulders shrugged. Amelia noted raised eyebrows and a few sniggers. Usual suspects, she thought.

"Please make sure." Amelia waited. Nothing. "If you come across it, please, please, please bring it to me right away." She quickly turned and clomped off toward the coffee bar, anxiety whispering in her ears.

In the short time she had worked for Sloane, Amelia had never lost her composure, and no one had ever seen her flustered. To all, she remained steady in the storm, even-keeled, unflappable. Especially with Sloane. This was how they had experienced her, so it was peculiar, an oddity really, this behavior of hers, this agitation, and it planted in everyone's mind the fast-germinating seed of curiosity. Like clover, it took root and sent out runners. It didn't take long for other thoughts to be crowded out by the desire to know about Sloane's note-book.

And then, a riot of reactions:

Charlotte chuckled. Amid quarterly profits and headcount numbers, the notebook probably contained grocery lists for Sloane's housekeeper, honey-dos for Harry, and other mundane stuff that Sloane would never wish to have disclosed for fear that it would clash with her persona. She must be apoplectic. Charlotte smiled. *This day is a gift.*

> If I thought there was power in those
> mantras she's always muttering, I'd
> speak them myself.

Holly couldn't imagine what the big deal was and ambled down the corridor to his next meeting. *It'll turn up.*

> Sometimes he looks like he's been up all
> night. Too many antacids. I worry.

There's nothing of great importance in my notebook, thought Vivian, but I still wouldn't want to lose it. Her mind flashed an image of Sloane writing intently in her notebook. She might mention the promotion … and if it's mine. She shook her head as if to clear it. All our privacies have been trespassed, and so little remains ours and solely ours. Even keep out signs don't keep them out. Sloane must certainly be upset. I don't blame her. I'll keep my eyes open.

What does she DO all of the time?

Dimitri immediately began to think of all the policies: confidentiality, disclosure, need-to-know, data privacy, secure communication, and access control. Someone finding, reading, and perhaps using or sharing information from Sloane's notebook would be in violation. The company held a strict view on internal confidentiality and disclosure. That's why it uses a variety of methods to monitor email, texts, and file access. He smiled. *There are possibilities here. I'll have a look around.*

Not bad to look at but better kept at a distance. Dangerously clever.

Baptiste noticed Amelia's nonverbal cues. *I bet there's something useful in that notebook, and I want to be the first to find it. I'll have a rummage.* He glanced at Alys.

He's a classic. An Iago in business attire, with a nose for opportunity that he can sniff out among the smell of sewage. And he's not afraid of getting soiled.

What a bother! I'm sure Sloane's concerned about the sensitive company stuff, thought Alys. That notebook likely contains some rather privileged information. I'm quite sure of it. Hmm. I wonder what could be so sensitive to have them both inflamed? Job cuts likely. But there must be more to it. I'll have a look around.

Fears the thing she's been hired to implement — change.

Jack immediately thought of himself and wondered if the promotion he so desperately wanted was mentioned in her notes. She hadn't yet said anything definitive, but who else? I'm her most ardent supporter. Her closest confidant. When she needs something, I'm here. And I actually like her. She has no better champion.

Jack can be such a fraud!

SLOANE

Sloane had a reputation for being redoubtable. She moved with the grace and power of a Friesian. This, paired with alabaster skin, cascading inky hair, and cornflower eyes that were sharp as blades, gave her a sense of mystery that she carried with a noble air. Her clothes were boxy and masculine in tailoring and yet she was undeniably feminine. Gold jewelry, Hermès scarves, and Stuart Weitzman stilettos were her trademarks.

She sat down, made room for her notebook to splay open unencumbered, and began to write.

> It will be a challenging week.
> Decisions made in favor of some will
> invariably cause pain for others.
> That's life — and reality.
> And they're not the same thing.

After reading *Harriet the Spy* at the age of 11, Sloane declared that she, too, would keep a notebook, spy on people, and grow up to be a writer. She had been cataloguing her thoughts ever since.

Her childhood spying flourished into keen observation capabilities and a sense for people, and their feelings and motivations. Instead of developing them as characters, she decided to help them develop as real people. And with that, she landed in what used to be called Personnel and was now elegantly billed as Human Resources — a function that most people found unexciting. But not Sloane.

Every now and again, she would raise a Bic pen to her mouth and press her tongue against the hole in the tip. It was the only pedestrian item she would tolerate besides the company-branded notebook. Everything else had to be luxury.

> It all starts with another team
> meeting. What will they bring back
> from last week's offsite? More hard
> feelings?! Or maybe — just maybe —
> a breakthrough...
>
> Charlotte was muttering to herself on
> the way in. As always. Wonder what
> her husband thinks about that ...
> mine would think me The Mad Hatter.

Sloane liked simplicity — the elegance of clean lines and the clarity of a well-organized space. She liked things to be streamlined: one notebook for all jottings, memos, and reminders. She didn't differentiate between her private musings about people and her business dealings. It all went into one notebook, which fit neatly into her bag and was available to her at any time. Her home office had shelves double stacked with the archives of her most recent volumes.

The last item took Sloane's mind to Jack and Vivian, both vying overzealously for a promotion. She pressed her lips together. Not subtle in their campaigning. Hard to think about promotions and cuts in the same week, but the world doesn't slow down or stop in order to make sense of things. Just no way around it.

She hated thinking about someone, anyone, losing their job, especially to meet a random budget cut percentage. It was a forced and careless exercise rather than an analytical or strategic one. What was it they said about the factory being torn down and rebuilt using the same logic? After some time, you'd find yourself right back where you started, at the same exercise. Sloane whispered a sigh into the inevitability of what lay ahead and then shifted and sat taller, as if the weight of the idea had thrust her down into her seat.

She shook her head, momentarily ridding herself of the hideous reality. Of course she would do it. She always did it. She'd cut a bit more or offer up a few more headcount, or some more money out of her budget. She would be recognized for her contributions and commitment to the company's success. She would be held up as an example of an enterprise leader, always doing more than her share, always looking beyond her own department, always the paragon — a word she liked.

Sloane arched her right brow as she looked up from her notebook. She couldn't see through the fog of her thoughts. She liked her team. All of them. They were quirky, in a good way, and different. They contrasted each other, which generally lends itself to advantage, though this group struggled. Amelia had been a good hire. Lots of drive, a strong spirit of inquiry, and loads of potential. Initially, Sloane held concern that Amelia hadn't stayed long in previous jobs — *young people these days!* — but they developed an easy and natural rapport when they met in person for Amelia's interview.

Sloane found Amelia stylish as she entered the conference room. Always a good first impression. Bold, in a red silk blouse, dark slim slacks, and pointed kitten heels. They soon discovered that a love of reading yoked them.

"Are you familiar with Maryse Condé?" Amelia asked. Whether or not someone had read her work was a mark of literary prowess in Amelia's eyes.

"Oh my, yes." Sloane couldn't believe her good fortune. "I have read everything she's written. Her work in English is a gift, and one that comes from the translator. You know it's her husband?"

"Yes, they're so symbiotic and produce such seamless work." Amelia's face brightened at the thought.

"Indeed." Sloane smiled. "Kazantzakis is also one of my favorites, though too obscure for many. And also Camus. Have you read them?"

They began to weave a tapestry of shared pleasure. Amelia praised Kafka, Austen, and Chopin, and on it went. Sloane made Amelia an offer that afternoon.

Sloane had long thought that it would be good to nurture and mentor Amelia. She had been doing so without having made it formal, but now it seemed she should give her idea some structure. It would serve Amelia well and add depth to her capabilities. Sloane thought that Amelia might be the lucky one to get this year's promotion. There's just one to give, and it could be hers. In Amelia there was a familiar echo.

Sloane's thoughts continued and periodically she would pause and jot something down. The weekend had been tense because Harry wouldn't stop complaining about her travel. He had expressed his displeasure before the offsite.

"Why do you have to take your team offsite, and out of town no less?" Harry shook his head slowly. "It's insensitive to the needs of their families."

"What are you talking about?" Sloane took a sharp breath.

"It's silly. And irresponsible. You're cutting budgets. You're going to be cutting jobs. These are turbulent times, and people need to be with their families. They need a level of normal in a time of change."

All Sloane could think was "What does he know?" He hadn't worked in a corporation, he hadn't been at her level in any organization, and he certainly didn't understand the needs of a team.

"Hosting a meeting," Sloane said, "that takes them away from home and office is a boost to morale, a secret pleasure." She gave a small nod affirming the thought. "Team offsites always begin with a veneer of camaraderie and polite tension. With skillful planning and the right exercises, people open up, they share, they become vulnerable, and then they bond. Competition takes a backseat, and they get closer. That's what I need these people to do." She stuck her neck forward and widened her eyes.

Harry let out a soft chuckle, then walked out, leaving Sloane staring after him.

At the offsite, she had noticed some friction between Jack and Vivian. Curious, she thought. And Dimitri's aura was slightly off, a change in his bearing. What could that mean? And Baptiste! So brazen sometimes! She wrote:

> Talk to Jack about Baptiste.
> Past his due date?

In her experience, cost cuts were a guise. Cleverly used they could eliminate a mounting issue. She advised leaders to do it all the time. She had done it herself. The team would breathe a sigh of relief. Baptiste was so. *What was he?* She looked up at the ceiling as if the right words might shake loose and descend. Patronizing. *That's polite, isn't it?* She chuckled. He's a lot of things. Arrogant. Vain. Can be cruel. Unfortunately, he's also creative and wise. Knows the right questions to ask, how to challenge assumptions, point us to what needs attention. All great leadership qualities, she thought. But how you treat people matters. And it affects results. *He has worn me out.* She almost said it aloud as if it were a declaration she was hearing for the first time. On one hand she liked him, but Baptiste bred resentment and that wasn't the right thing to propagate.

Sloane glanced at her Cartier Tank and closed her notebook. She flashed back to childhood, reading her beloved Harriet over and over — her most affectionate memories. The corners of her mouth turned upward. Sloane shunned all the business literature that swirled around the office and promised the cure for leadership, culture, strategy, and everything that ails corporations and the people in them. Instead, she was nourished by unexpected stories of people navigating and living life. Colorful characters laughing, loving, crying, overcoming. And sometimes they simply failed. Fate had its way. Literature was Sloane's steadfast mentor. It was her Ole Gollie.

She gathered her things and headed for the conference room.

Team Meeting

The meeting began just as the snow intensified, both set off by an inaudible chime, like a dog whistle. The flakes twirled as did the rising chatter in the conference room. They were nine around the long white table. Notebooks, laptops, and phones scattered out in front of each of them. Charlotte and Vivian shared a moment of understanding, leaning into each other. Dimitri scrolled through his phone, rarely looking up. The rest talked, heads ping-ponging as the words sailed across the room. Sloane sat at the head, as always. Amelia sat next to her.

The wall behind Sloane was lined with books sitting spine out. All the best-selling organizational titles occupied shelf space, from *The Five Dysfunctions of a Team* to *The Fifth Discipline* to *Reinventing Organizations*. Everything by Block, Schein, and Galbraith sat waiting. The selection was so large that newer titles stood in stacks on the credenza. It was a well-read library and yet the knowledge within had never found full employment.

Sloane spoke and everyone took notes. "There is pressure to cut costs. That shouldn't come as a surprise. We'll need to keep next year's budget flat and look at projects and what we can put off or trim."

"We could shift some monies if needed," said Jack.

"And you know what that means," said Vivian, sweeping her gaze across the room as she suppressed a groan.

"We'll also need to review headcount. No one has said anything about reductions, but we should expect they will," Sloane said.

"The market is getting increasingly competitive and tight," said Holly, and then he sighed.

"It could mean salary inflation," Dimitri exhaled the last word slowly as he flashed a smug grin and took a sip of his coffee.

Sloane rested her eyes on him for a long second, and then continued, "Talent is needed. It's always needed. In my experience, a good place to find it is in our competitors. People bring knowledge and resources that could prove beneficial."

"It's such a contradiction." Charlotte spoke up. "Cuts and hires. Cuts and hires. You know how this looks to the organization. Here we go again."

"Come on Charlotte," said Jack. "You heard Sloane. It's coming from the top. Things are tight. Things are competitive. We've got to cut to get ahead. We can do this."

Alys, always the martyr, found a sword, fell on it, and bled all over the table. "We can't treat people like this. It's so unfair. The company doesn't care about people. It only cares about itself. Why do the employees have to pay the price? This is just another example of bad planning on the part of senior leaders."

"We are senior leaders," Sloane reminded her.

Holly ate an antacid out of a plastic baggy, and his hand lingered as if another might be needed.

The other tongues remained silent.

What was striking about the scene was the conformity. Everyone used the same notebook with the company logo on the bottom right. Everyone used a Bic pen, though some preferred blue to black, and Dimitri used red. Every phone was enclosed in a black case with the same embossed emblem. All ear pods were white. All computers were Apple. Everything was company issue. Holly and Dimitri wore shirts with the company logo. They were like Penelope's suitors, mistaking access for entitlement.

What varied were the personalities. Amelia looked around thinking: *This a superfund site — though no potential for remediation*. Pleasantries overflowed, but everyone, while different as fire and ice, shared the kinship of ruthlessness. All sought individual advancement, a natural human tendency, but here it was relentlessly pursued, through optics more than ability, many driven to check all the right boxes. More importantly, the focus was on the endgame: to surpass, eclipse, outmaneuver on the way to the top.

Assessing a new job or workplace requires time. For Amelia, it only took a few weeks to gauge the team. She ran the numbers like a bookie trying to determine if she would place a longer-term bet. Baptiste was easy to unmask, inflating his own sense of superiority, strutting like a peacock. To him, everyone was a commodity. Holly was worth a wager: seasoned from experience, gentle, patient, not fully retired-in-place but certainly waiting out the time clock. Dimitri: calculating. Alys: spoiled. Vivian and Charlotte, in their own ways, offered riches to the team but were overlooked: one because she wore her contributions like a sandwich board, and the other because she spoke in hushed tones. And then there was Jack. If he was slightly smaller, he'd be a lapdog. And of course, there was Sloane.

Amelia had observed the team: multiple emails sent between team members that received no response, forceful shutting of laptops at the end of work sessions, whispering in the coffee bar, and the darting of eyes to read incoming texts as meetings dragged. She knew, once again, that this would not be a long-term assignment. It would, however, do for now. She liked Sloane, though she didn't trust her. She had witnessed several occasions when Sloane changed her story or found ways to pass off accountability. For all Sloane's admirable courage and confidence, there was a measure of cravenness. Sometimes people were just too hard to reconcile.

GATHERING

The room was airless. They stood and huddled around a flip chart to conduct a retrospective of the prior week's offsite. Holly suddenly became aware of their mingling scents — jasmine, lavender, sandalwood, apple, sea breeze. The combination was oppressive, and he stepped back from the crowd. Alys thought this a pointless exercise, another façade no different than last week's hollow attempt at teamwork. She withdrew to lean against the wall. The others clustered close to Sloane. Charlotte murmured to herself.

Anyone passing down the corridor, looking in through the glass, might falsely think the gathering was convivial. The group plumed themselves, leaning in slightly, nodding as each spoke. Jack smoothed his shirt, running his right hand down and up the fabric, resting it over his heart for a few seconds and then pointing and gesturing. Baptiste held his steepled fingers against his lips, and occasionally threw Alys a look. Vivian laughed a bit too much and a bit too loud, and she would reach and lightly touch an arm in response to a statement. Dimitri adjusted his cuffs. Sloane, overly gracious in her praise, reworded or clarified everything into finality.

Sloane presided. She always repeated her opinions: "That's our top priority and we need to marshal our resources." Always pushed away ideas she disliked: "I don't see the value in that." Always decided the outcome: "Good discussion and perspectives. We'll do as Alys has suggested." Always spoke the last word: "That's quite a list. We're at a good stopping point." And always accepted the accolades for her leadership: "I appreciate that! Thank you. I love leading this team." Small victories held value. But her desire to win was not about contest. It was about the attention that would be showered upon her for having won. She craved admiration.

Sloane glanced at the clock, skillfully summarized the conversation and decisions made, and called the meeting to a close: "Let's make it a great week."

SLOANE

Despite her successes, Sloane was parched for admiration.

It began in childhood. Her parents were university professors. Her mother: a tall, willowy art historian with a specialty in *Die Brücke* that frequently transported her to Berlin. Her father: a trade policy wonk with a broad chest, zestful laugh, and brawny arms with which he dispensed hugs and slaps on the back. As well as academia, he spent time in several think tanks, and when he wasn't immersed in economic study, he spoke at conferences or appeared as a guest on broadcasts. Sloane's parents were loving but distant, preoccupied with their own passions, never fully aware of the needs of their only, and lonely, child.

> They were out again tonight. Some
> boring lecture. They'll come home and
> want to talk about it. On and on.
> Hopefully there'll be time to talk about
> my science project.
> Mrs. Holiday LOVED it.

When asked, Sloane spoke fondly of her parents and her upbringing. Though somewhat emotionally neglected, she did receive a bounty of gifts from her mother and father, and considered her early life to have been happy.

> I'm lucky to have my mom and dad.
> We laugh a lot, when they are here
> anyway. At Jordan's house they don't.
> His parents are getting a divorce. His
> father has already moved out. It's sad.

Sloane's parents modeled ideals that she quietly noticed and absorbed. One word stuck out to her — respect. Her mother and father spoke of it often, in different ways, both in how to give it and how to earn it. Sloane came to understand that it was important, and she grew into her understanding of how foundational it would be to her life.

> Mom and Dad are always talking about
> respect. They respect a lot of people. And
> their opinions. I'm kinda starting to
> understand what they mean when they
> say they respect differences or choices
> and even decisions.

Faced with typical childhood challenges, Sloane sought out her mother and confided fears, longings, and questions. Her mother responded with the tools she knew best: art and literature. Pressure at school to conform: her mother suggested Sloane read *Stargirl*. Wonderings about self and identity: her mother showed photos of Rodin's *Thinker* and Picasso's *Girl Before a Mirror*. Questioning the actions of other kids: her mother bought Sloane a copy of *Each Kindness*. To teach her independence and perseverance: her mother asked her to analyze Winslow Homer's *The Gulf Stream*.

I can always count on Mom. She
knows everything – and just the right
thing when I need it. Like when she
showed me this painting of people all
lined up on a riverbank, dressed
really proper, barely moving.
She said it was beautiful, and it was,
but it was also a bunch of stiff people
looking like they were trying not to
wrinkle their clothes. It reminded me
of those times I get so caught up in
standing just right, saying the right
thing, acting like someone people
would approve of.
I think that was her point. Sometimes
I try too hard to be what I'm supposed
to be and forget to just be myself.

Sloane became a voracious reader, and her world grew. She discovered that books could contain her thoughts: some having been already written in the novels she read, and others that she catalogued in her notebook.

Even though she felt her parents' love, her thirst remained unquenched. She decided that respect, which was so important to her parents, would be her ultimate aim.

> I want to be respected. Mom and Dad
> pay attention to people they respect.
> They talk about them. Respect is
> important to them. Respect will mean
> Mom and Dad and others will pay
> attention to me.

To get it, Sloane turned elsewhere. She broadened her interests, and participated in competitions. She excelled at everything. While the tributes came flooding to her, there remained a dry spot for validation and affirmation from her parents. They were always delighted, yet they remained busy and preoccupied. Their accolades seemed fleeting.

Sloane remained in pursuit, but over time she hardened. The once solid convictions bestowed by her parents gave way to compromises she felt were required to keep the acclaim flowing.

> Mom and Dad were happy about Mr.
> Cunningham's praise of my essay.

I told them all about it and what
happened at school. I left out the part
about Melanie's essay being considered the most creative.

She learned pretense and became skilled at putting on a performative voice and smile.

There are so many boors in my
Medieval Lit class. So full of themselves. Our yearbook editor asked my
opinion of the class, and I just smiled
and said...

She began to bias decisions in her favor and to select favor-ites among friends and colleagues.

I decided to give the promotion to
Leona. She's really good but lacks
ambition. That will work in my favor
over time: no competition.

She gossiped and changed stories or sides when it was con-venient to her desired outcomes.

The head of Finance came in to
complain about Zia. I listened.

I smiled. And then I agreed with
everything he had to say. I need him
on my side, and if he sees the situation this way, then I do too. I'll get on
Zia about this tomorrow. I can't have
this behavior.

Her accountability flagged, and she made excuses for herself or blamed others.

That Baptiste. He accused me of
changing my story. It's the facts that
have changed, not my story. I'm just
telling it like it is. He needs to be more
diligent.

The changes were small and infrequent, yet over time they
shifted from conscious action to habit. The deficits of her upbringing had cast a long shadow, and it followed her into marriage, parenthood, and career.

CHARLOTTE

Charlotte inhaled deeply as she stepped out of the elevator. As a ritual, she silently reviewed her motivations and what she hoped to achieve. Her husband, Samuel, was growing a car rental business, and changes in technology required the steady upgrade of his fleet. He also needed more staff. Until now he had juggled many of the responsibilities himself. Their three daughters were all in college, each a year apart, a testament to a love that had never waned in physical attraction. Undergraduate degrees today were the high school diplomas of prior decades, and graduate school loomed for all. Everything, it seemed, was taking longer. The house in the mountains would have to wait. *I'm making my dreams a reality*, she reminded herself.

She walked down the corridor, toward the open space, and asked herself the round of questions she had accumulated from years of leadership development training. She answered with the mantras that energized her. She paused slightly between the call and the response:

Where do I focus my time and energy this week?
I will concentrate on what has tangible impact.

What can I do to make my goals easier?
> *I keep things simple and nourish myself with healthy choices.*

How do I continuously elevate my leadership?
> *I turn every challenge into a chance to learn and grow.*

Charlotte favored the workspace next to the window. She preferred to sit there because of the natural light and the view of the trees. She looked outside. Snow fell. She unloaded her tote bag and headed for her locker. She returned a few minutes later with a cup of black coffee, a rainbow-colored stack of post-its, and a zippered pouch with markers. She unfurled the flip chart pages from last week's offsite and laid them on the ground. It took a few minutes to reorient to what was written and to the context of the conversations that had taken place. She had offered to streamline the notes as there were a few ideas she advocated, and this was a way to emphasize them.

The offsite had devoured a week that she would rather have spent on something else. It lasted four full days, with travel on both sides. She was wiped out by the second day. Too many people. Too much togetherness. They started with breakfast and went on into the evening. While this was standard, she had hoped for time to herself and devised excuses to briefly escape whenever she could.

Boundaries are healthy and do not require explanation.

A course for emerging leaders early in her career had birthed Charlotte's belief in the power of mantra. For her, they held the same power as prayer, and positive thinking. Reality was what you made of it. With the right focus, positive energy would flow. Like would attract like. Negative currents would remain at bay. The only thing one can control is self. She believed in all of it.

Just before nine o'clock, she went to the coffee bar for a refill and then headed to the conference room. A blur of snow was descending. It was Monday, and the team meeting was about to begin.

She returned an hour later to rekindle the work on the offsite recap, when shortly thereafter Amelia called everyone to attention. Her voice was fractured. Her eyes wide. Sloane had lost her notebook. Big deal, thought Charlotte, there's a supply closet full of them. No one seemed to have it, and Amelia appeared to sink with the realization. *If I thought it contained something that jeopardized my job, I'd be concerned.* Charlotte's eyes flickered and her mouth twisted as she imagined Sloane's displeasure. She then quickly frowned at what she thought it might translate into for Amelia. *Not good.*

"Tell me who you are" was Sloane's first volley upon meeting Charlotte. It was a different tactic than "Tell me about yourself." Slight but significant. Sloane had scored, and their relationship flourished with ease.

Their individual narratives shared similar plot points. Both married young. Motherhood came early enough that it posed no professional obstacle. Their husbands supported their ambitions, and mentors helped advance their careers.

There was much to like about Sloane. She had a pleasant voice, was quick to laugh, and demonstrated a sharp wit. She loved to read and in team meetings would often mention her latest literary discovery.

In a crisis, she would square her shoulders and stand tall, breathing evenly, speaking in clear, measured statements. Faced with an emotional employee, she would maintain empathetic eye contact while speaking in a low, soothing, and reassuring manner. She listened and acknowledged while nodding gently and offering a warm smile. When a meeting or a gathering seemed to be floundering, she would take the lead by reaffirming its purpose, guiding the discussion, and keeping dialogue moving.

She was easy to like.

Over time, however, Charlotte witnessed contradictions. Sloane might advise her to proceed one way in a matter, and then state something different publicly or to the rest of the team. If someone influential brought a concern, Sloane sided with them even if she had been the source of said concern. On a handful of occasions, Sloane blatantly said the opposite of what she had said in a prior conversation. Confronted, she would deny it without the blink of an eye or a flush of the cheeks.

The instances were few, but Charlotte realized that Sloane should not and could not be trusted. It saddened her. Not only because of what Sloane had done, but more so because from then on, Charlotte would have to be careful. Being on guard was energy that she would have to redirect — not out of fear, but to preserve the equilibrium she worked so hard to create.

Charlotte did not, however, change her demeanor, and her caution was imperceptible to Sloane. The rest of the team continued to think them close, and Sloane still openly confided in Charlotte.

They invariably discussed Baptiste at length, and Charlotte relished every morsel as gossip. Baptiste inspired either devotion or repulsion, and opinions were firmly set. Charlotte despised him.

For reasons she could not fathom, Baptiste wanted nothing to do with her. The wall between them, impenetrable. The disdain he carried, blatant. She often told Samuel that if Baptiste were a knife, she would have run out of blood. Her only solace: she wasn't the only one.

Vivian was the other object of Baptiste's apathy. Unlike Charlotte, she tried to make Baptiste acknowledge her, make eye contact with her, speak to her. Charlotte found it embarrassing. Partly because it didn't work, and partly because public dismissal was so demeaning. *I focus on what I can control.*

Vivian was another constant in her conversations with Sloane. She puzzled Sloane and Charlotte. "I don't get her," Sloane had repeatedly said. "What does she do all the time?" It was a valid question and one that Charlotte couldn't and didn't want to answer. *I release all thoughts that drain me and bring me down.*

Vivian always worked late, always asked for more resources, always crowed about how much she had done and how little she was recognized for it. It was a tired tune, and her record kept skipping. At her level, it was unusual and professionally immature. Charlotte wanted to broach it with Vivian, to see if she could bring about some relief or ease the burden of what appeared to be overwork, and she attempted to do so on several occasions. She also wanted to learn something, anything, that she could quietly pass to Sloane. But Vivian preferred reasons, excuses, and complaints. She rehashed the past in minute detail to make a point – Holly was given her headcount two years ago, Alys had two assistants while she only had one, collaborating with Jack meant receiving actions at the last minute, and on it went. Charlotte abandoned any notion of being helpful and continued to grouse with Sloane.

They metered out praise as well as judgment, casting a wide net across the team.

Charlotte viewed Amelia as a refreshing addition. The last admin had thought she had landed in a den of snakes and suffered from too many bites. With no antidote, she transferred to another team.

Charlotte had never seen Amelia flustered like she was this morning. *It couldn't just be that notebook.* Amelia's pedigree was interesting for an admin — a Literature major, maybe with a minor in Classics? She couldn't quite recall. She and Sloane loved reading and were always exchanging book titles. Charlotte had taken a few recommendations but thought their tastes were a bit highbrow. *Hour of the Star? Really?*

This spring will mark her eleventh year at the company. She had only planned to stay for three to five and then go find something else, but she's steadfast about her goals and continues to see a manageable path to achieve them by staying put. Charlotte has outlived a handful of Sloanes. And Baptistes. And Vivians. There have been worse, and there have been better. She maintains a healthy distance from her colleagues. She's friendly and well-liked, makes jokes, and lingers in the coffee bar to talk about the latest Netflix series, bitcoin, or what's going on with X. *I am resilient and strong.*

Charlotte downplays her abilities, and her colleagues fall for it every time, praising her accomplishments and marveling at her seemingly endless capacity to excel. Sloane always gives her an exceptional rating, and a special something extra in her comp statement. Charlotte understands the power of understatement — a concept foreign to her colleagues. *I am grateful for my blessings.*

Shortly after the team meeting, Charlotte went back to the conference room to make some notes from the flip charts they had just created. She sat and twirled the chair to face the easel, bent down to adjust her shoe, when she spotted it wedged underneath the credenza. She thought that it likely had fallen off the table and gotten kicked aside in the shuffle of feet. Charlotte dislodged it and opened the front flap. There was no name or information in the space for "In case of loss," but there was a quote — "Better a thousand enemies outside the house than one inside." *Ah! Shakespeare. Good grief!*

She rose to go and take the notebook to Amelia and then stopped. There would be too many questions, and she had other things to do. An easy resolution was to take it to the copy room and find an obvious place to lay it to rest. Amelia was often in there straightening up.

Typing...

Amelia: I found something in the copy room

Sloane: My notebook?

Amelia: No, but perhaps a copy of some pages — looks like thoughts about someone who was let go, but it doesn't say who — this might be the last page of it and was accidentally left behind

Sloane: ???

Amelia: Makes no sense

Sloane: Take a picture and text it

Amelia: Will do

Sloane: I don't get it

Sloane: It means someone is going through it!!

Amelia: Will keep looking — Wanted you to be aware — Will send pic in a sec

Baptiste

When he came across the notebook, it was around noon. Baptiste could see nothing beyond the windows as he walked down the corridor, only a shroud of snow. He stopped at the file room on his way back to his desk and was gobsmacked to see the notebook so casually displayed on the corner of one of the cabinets. Even at first glance, he was certain that it was Sloane's, and a slow smile crept across his face.

Heavy footfalls approached just as he reached for his bit of luck, and he turned in time to see Vivian hurry past. *Stupid cow!* He sneered.

She had startled him, but even if he were caught with it, who would know that it wasn't his? *She* certainly wouldn't dare question him. Besides, he thought, I'm a good actor. And indeed, he was.

Drama had been part of his school curriculum in England, and he supplemented that learning with workshops and summer school at RADA. His grandmother underwrote what she recognized as his passion and imagined someday seeing him on a stage in the West End. However, his parents were neutral about his acting, harboring more traditional visions of his future in medicine or academia.

One day, Baptiste announced to his father that he would become an actor and had decided to attend RADA full-time after school. This declaration caused his father to emphatically proclaim that no child who sprang from his loins would spend his professional career on stage, whether he had been trained at the Royal Academy or not. The decision was final. Made for him, not by him. Baptiste had always assumed he'd have the freedom to decide his future, particularly with his parents repeated encouragement to consider his prospects and be the one to shape his own destiny. But he knew now that they only liked the idea of his adulthood, not the reality of it.

Baptiste knew his father would never relent. Outwardly, he used his acting training to mask his grief and disillusionment, playing his part with ease. Inwardly, he stood bare on the stage, recalling Shakespeare and craving the fullness of life — love, loss, betrayal, and all things that made him feel human and real. These experiences came to him only on stage, and he knew that if he became a barrister or an accountant, he would not be able to escape the numbness of a life unlived.

To his father, Baptiste agreed to pursue a business career. But he vowed to himself that this would not stop him from performing.

The notebook fell open, and Baptiste's eye landed on the words "busybodies, ingrates, egomaniacs, liars, the jealous, and cranks." He smiled. *So that's what she thinks of us.* There were comments about people, but there weren't names associated. Who or what were they? "The silent guardian, the obsequious opportunist, the productive loner." His thoughts ran laps. "Oh, I see," he said aloud. "They're epithets. Well, I've got one for you, my lady. I'd call you The Yea-and-Nay Leader."

He flipped to another page and found an organization chart of their team and a drawing of the solar system. Interesting, he thought. Same information, different imagery. It was clear that Sloane was the sun. Of course, thought Baptiste. What an imagination! He found his name at Jupiter. *What a cow!* Jack was Mercury. The little sycophant. Alys was next. No surprise, he thought. He heard plodding footsteps again, snapped the notebook shut, tucked it under his arm, turned and walked out the door where he almost ran straight into Vivian. He made a disgusted sound and didn't stop. Vivian would swear that he told her to sod off. She's such a nobody, he thought, and he realized he didn't see to which planet she had been assigned.

Later in the day, while reflecting on the placement of their named orbs, he came to realize the opportunity he lost. He seethed knowing that he should have kept the notebook longer instead of hastily depositing it into the kitchen. "That notebook, he muttered to himself, is a hoard of secrets waiting to be exploited." In this environment, currency existed in many forms — alliances, influence, knowledge. In a word: leverage. He smirked. Information is currency, and that notebook is a jackpot.

He mused about what he might have learned from Sloane's views of Alys. A bit of dirt on Holly or Dimitri wouldn't hurt either. And Jack — a few crumbs about Jack would be quite tasty. What else could be in that notebook? Amelia was quite put out. *Blimey, there must be something damning in there.* Once again, his thoughts drifted to the planets. Power is certainly about positioning, and Jack is in the choicest spot. Alys was close too. Quite the prize, that Alys. And his thoughts immediately portered him back to last week's offsite.

Baptiste relished a good monologue even if its performance was only in his head:

> *Fortune is the only mistress that I've ever had.*
> *They say she can be fickle, but never with me.*
> *I learned to court her long ago.*
> *She yielded to my advances,*
> *and she's been partial to me ever since.*

He continued: We understand each other. She likes that I am bold. I like that she is lavish. Together we're a power couple. In fact, it was Fortune who pointed me to the riches of the Alys conquest. Spoils indeed. I hadn't ever considered Alys anything other than mild competition, a man hater, and someone exceedingly needy. I certainly didn't find her attractive. It's Dimitri who catches my eye. But there she was: an opportunity. And when opportunity knocks, I don't just open the door. I invite her in. I open my arms, and I embrace her. Because ultimately, I will exploit every ounce of her. Exactly as I did with Alys.

Baptiste shifted his stance and held his head erect, elongating his neck.

He continued his silent monologue: All great art and all great artists enter at the wound. And that's where I started. It was easy really. She'd had too much to drink. We both had. But my tolerance is better, and midway through the evening I quietly signaled the bartender to stop adding vodka to my tonic. I began to peel away the layers as I would her clothing later in the evening.

"Why do you hate men?" Until then our banter had been superficial. The others had slowly trickled out and up to their rooms. The day had been long. Only Amelia was left, sitting at the bar in conversation with the handsome bartender. I turned back to Alys.

"I don't hate men — I just think they are advantaged unfairly, and I'm tired of it." She sat up straight and looked directly into my eyes. She was expecting something.

"Have you been disadvantaged?" I leaned in.

"Only because of my brother. It's never happened otherwise. I won't allow it." She slouched back in her chair. She had been prepared for something else.

"Disadvantage has a will of his own. It's not always up to you to allow it."

"No." She looked away and then back at Baptiste. "You're right. But I won't allow it when I have a say in it. And I will not allow white men to continue to enjoy their gender privilege, higher salaries, and kudos for being assertive. Women don't get that."

"You're always making cracks like that about men, white men in particular."

"That makes you safe."

"Poor Jack though. You target him the most."

"He's a Sloane favorite, and that also leads to advantage."

"Interesting." Baptiste chuckled. "So, what happened with your brother?"

"Typical stuff, father's favorite, mother's favorite, couldn't do any wrong, excelled at many things but not all, was always given a pass, stole all of the light."

"And all of the love?" Baptiste feigned a pout.

She shook her head. "I didn't have a bad childhood. My parents are good people. They love me. I love them. My brother too. They provided a very comfortable upbringing for us. We had everything. I just felt they were unfair. That's why I've tried to be fair with my boys."

"But they're boys. How can you raise boys and hate men? That is what they'll become."

"I want them to become men that respect women. Starting with girls."

He continued: And that's how our conversation began to unfold. Like a dance. I took the lead, and then she did. We passed it back and forth fluidly, moving with the rhythm of the words and motion of our thoughts. She was sharp-tongued and spirited, and she threw her head back when she was pleased with a point she made. When I spoke, she listened attentively, and her facial expressions revealed her reactions. I found myself surprised, genuinely engaged, and most assuredly titillated. She had opened the door, and I simply walked through it.

I wasn't smitten. That is a luxury for those who are *not* seducers. My attraction was layered, intentional, and manipulative. I certainly hadn't expected it to be so easy. And I certainly hadn't expected to enjoy myself. I typically maintained distance from Alys. She's loud in meetings and can suck all the air out of the room. Sloane favors her – speaking of advantage — and that makes us competitors regardless of skill or talent or comparison.

To get some of what I wanted, I turned the conversation back to Jack and the team, and that led to an outpouring of gossip that I relished and stored for future use.

"It's obvious to everyone, and not just me, that Jack is vying for a promotion." Baptiste smiled. *This we all can see, since he is as subtle and annoying as a pimple.*

Alys nodded and laughed and said that Jack's wife was the one with the more prominent career. "She's a patent attorney. Also a mother of three. And she runs marathons. And plays the flute." She paused between phrases for effect.

Baptiste had known nothing of Jack's wife. He found this new narrative rather delicious, and he practically smacked his lips.

"I'm serious," continued Alys. "She's superhuman this lady. I don't know how she does it."

"And Jack, on the other hand," Baptiste said. "Is a mediocre bureaucrat, making his way to the top by picking up Sloane's leftovers and handouts while nodding his head 'yes.' Sloane likes him because he flatters her — and everyone else above him."

Alys's mouth slowly broadened into a smile, and her eyes danced in agreement. Baptiste leaned back in his seat and returned a grin.

The monologue continued: Jack wrote the playbook on managing up. His biggest asset is his face. The second, his ass. Other than that, not interesting. I imagine he's got a complex about not being as good or accomplished as his wife – which I find pitiful and loathsome really. Poor Jack, he is overshadowed by all her feats. His sad story added a few more coins to my bank. In my opinion, he's not that motivated. He's one of those guys who lacks real ambition, but he's found his niche and has been successful with it. A cowardly yes man if you ask me. But yes, a nice ass.

Baptiste inhaled to a count of four, held his breath for seven seconds, and exhaled until he had nothing left to expel.

Oh Alys. He smiled. Yes, where were we?

Ah yes, ladders. Whether the corporate ladder or Jacob's ladder, you'll find rungs that lead upward to match the aspirations of those on the ascent. Jack and Vivian are both climbing, and both are toadying to Sloane. Alys had interesting insight into Vivian, but I was only half-listening as I don't care about that woman. She grates on me, and I don't have time for people like her who drain energy rather than provide any value. At our level, you don't get ahead by crying about what you lack. She'd be more interesting if she talked about what she accomplished and how she added value. To be honest, I don't even know if she does.

He inhaled again.

Back to Alys. She doesn't care about getting a promotion — or so she says. She's content, does what she wants, disappears when she wants. She's got a side hustle, a consulting practice she's building for the future, and she spends a lot of her time on it. I didn't know, but I'm surprised Sloane hasn't noticed. I filed that knowledge away. More coins in my bank.

I also learned that Charlotte is not held in as high esteem as I believed. She is by some, but Sloane has shared with Alys that Charlotte has plateaued. Sloane has spoken differently to me about Charlotte. Hence the Yea-and-Nay. Typical Sloane. Personally, I've never understood Charlotte's appeal. She manages to be competent and yet entirely unremarkable. I'm not so arrogant as to think I can't learn from others, but she offers nothing but a stream of mutterings dressed up as insights. She adds no value. At least not to me.

Alys and I spared no one. We went around the conference table and praised and skewered our colleagues. We wounded and bandaged and produced lots of scars. It was quite fun really.

It turns out that Alys is quite fond of Sloane. I'd always viewed their relationship as very parent-child. And now that I know more, I see that Sloane gives Alys the attention that Alys's parents gave to her brother, and Alys gives Sloane loyalty, reverence, and a lot of attention and praise.

If I'm honest, I have to admit that Sloane is a great leader, and there is much in her success that I admire. But I don't like her. She is a shapeshifter when it comes to the truth, and she adjusts her sails with every gust of wind. To challenge her is to expect penalties — which she will deliver with a stone face. Make no mistake, she is every bit the boss. In the game of politics, she is a force to be reckoned with. And while I greatly dislike her, I also greatly admire her skill.

On a few occasions during my conversation with Alys, I turned back to her family, her childhood, and her career. I was careful in my probing, interested in gathering as much information as possible. I flattered her with frequency. She didn't just take the bait. She swallowed it and practically burped with glee.

I was struck at how she held herself in reserve throughout our dialogue in the bar, but when we stumbled into her hotel room, she was completely unguarded. As I exposed her body, she exposed herself. She was inflamed, and she was pliable.

But seduction isn't just about physical attraction. It's about understanding desires and vulnerabilities, and how to best leverage them to your advantage. Our dance was delicate. Forward. Backward. Chasse. It's about creating an illusion of desire, making the other person believe it's their idea, setting the stage for them to succumb to want.

The last time I had sex with a woman, it was my 20th birthday. An unrestrained party, a lot of alcohol, and a 24-year-old with long limbs and loose hair the color of bread. I thought it might be the last time, but I didn't want to lock myself into a fixed definition of my sexuality. I didn't want to be pinned to a wall like a butterfly, labeled and trapped.

I gave up the freedom to be myself once — to my father — and I vowed to never do it again.

That Alys, she was too good to pass up though. And while I hadn't ever found her attractive, I did find myself wanting her. So, I decided to be with a woman again.

JACK

Jack had a secret, and it involved arousal.

He watched his neighbor every morning from his third-floor window. She was a German brunette with shapely legs. An open courtyard sat in the center of the city block which they shared, and his building stood on the north side with his kitchen window overlooking the manicured boxwoods and well-groomed azaleas that populated their quadrangle. His was a direct line of sight across and down to her bedroom window, and she always left her curtains open — even as she dressed for work.

Jack paused his thoughts. *Why am I thinking about my neighbor?* He smiled. It was the arousal of curiosity, and it triggered him in the same way as seeing her in her panties. His mind zig-zagged momentarily. I didn't understand why there was such a flutter about the notebook. Amelia was almost accusatory about its whereabouts, and said Sloane was in a lather. Now, I have seen Sloane lose her shit, he thought, but over a notebook? *Come. On.* He was immediately intrigued. Something wicked had to be between those pages, and that aroused him even more.

He thought again about his neighbor. *Mmm.* She must know that I watch. A pulse stirred within, and he quickly willed it away.

Jack was easily aroused. From a young age, he possessed a strong sense of desire — a perpetual hard-on not uncommon to growing boys, one that stayed with him into adulthood. In high school and college, he found himself in the popular crowd, but he wasn't the one the girls had their hearts set on. He wasn't unattractive. He made people laugh, always carried a smile, and was endlessly adaptable, but he wasn't *that* guy. While his buddies went after the girls everyone crushed on, he ended up with their overlooked friends, the ones also overflowing with hormones, hoping someone would notice them. Invariably, he found himself making out with a girl because he needed a release. Initially, he was disappointed that he would never date the prom queen or the head cheerleader, but he quickly realized that the girls, like him, who tagged along were easier to get, certainly eager, and essentially an untapped reservoir. He reasoned that he could be happy with castoffs. His position in the circle afforded perks — tickets to the Mets game, an invitation to a private lecture, a quick blowjob in the bathroom. Every girl wanted a guy, and he learned to be *that* guy for many. He had lots of sex and a fair number of girlfriends, and he discovered that picking up someone else's crumbs wasn't so bad after all.

Jack never shared his secret in the telling sense, but he did share it. She's blind to what I'm doing, he thought. He grinned at how much he loved his morning ritual. He watched and sipped his cup of coffee as he leaned against the counter, and when his Fräulein had departed for work, he quietly went back to bed and gently woke his wife. As everyone knew, Jack adored his wife. He thought an active sex life was the sign of a strong marriage, and after twenty-two years, they we're still getting after it like rabbits, as Jack would brag to his friends.

Stop, he thought. He couldn't think about his German delight while at the office or else he'd have to find a place to relieve the pressure.

And then.

A fleeting moment of awe accompanies every new discovery. Jack experienced it as he entered the coffee bar and saw the notebook laying there waiting. If he were of different character, he would have been conflicted, at minimum momentarily. But he wasn't. He was drawn to it like iron to a magnet. He supposed that he might find Sloane's notes about the team, perhaps performance feedback from interviews, possibly some math around compensation. Performance season had arrived, and the notebook might contain an indication about his promotion. Jack and Sloane had worked closely together for many years, confiding in one another and, at times, completing each other's sentences. They enjoyed a professional intimacy that could be misinterpreted by others as favoritism, but he appreciated the partnership and the unique underlying friendship. With him, Sloane was unguarded, openly praising and openly criticizing others. Generally, he agreed with her, but sometimes he didn't, and in these instances, he remained silent. After all, she was the boss.

While Sloane was loose with her opinions and a great deal of information, she had lines she would not cross. Sharing news of a promotion or raise before it was official was one of them. He knew she'd leave no trail, no hint, remaining close-mouthed about it until it happened. And he was fairly certain it would. *I know how to act surprised. Just keep moving me up the ladder, Sloane, keep giving me more money, keep making me more visible. One day, I'll be your replacement.*

Like a comet, Alys abruptly streaked across his mind. *What if she gets the promotion instead?* Anything was possible. Absurd, but possible. Jack and Alys were close even though she often stung him about being a white male, going on and on about double standards, gender privilege, and patriarchy. The only thing she hadn't done was call him a misogynist. He always and easily dismissed her comments. Gender equality was an issue he cared deeply about, but he wasn't going to be guilt tripped into anything, certainly not by Alys and certainly not with his background of promoting women. He thought Alys misguided and knew Sloane didn't fall for moral exhibitionism.

He was slightly rattled, and his thoughts turned to Baptiste. *What a bastard,* Jack thought as he started to open the notebook. He got the promotion last year instead of me. *He's such a brown noser.* Jack quietly fumed. And then Amelia came in, and he instinctively closed the notebook and tucked it under his arm.

"Any news on the search?"

"No, not yet. Everyone is in and out of meetings, so I haven't been able to talk to people individually." She gave him a hard look.

"Well, good luck with the sleuthing."

She nodded and began to load the dishwasher. Jack walked out, the notebook pushing into his ribs. He would do nothing to jeopardize his promotion, and he walked directly to Amelia's desk, where he laid the notebook on the corner. It was four o'clock.

Typing...

Sloane: Any news?

Amelia: Not yet

Amelia: Who is Xavier Montgomery?

Sloane: R&D, why?

Amelia: His name was on a sticky in the file room, perhaps someone was looking for his file?

Sloane: ? Everything is electronic

Amelia: Strange…

Amelia: Anything about him in your notebook?

Amelia could see that Sloane was typing, but her response was slow in coming.

Sloane: I need you to find my notebook

Sloane: Just let me know when you have it

HOLLY

Holly came across it in the coffee bar. It was about three o'clock. To him, the notebook was as hot as a stovepipe. By early afternoon, Sloane stalked the corridors, going back and forth to meetings, fists and teeth clenched, her anger radiating. Holly guessed it was the missing journal, but recognized it could also be the content of some of the day's meetings. In the morning elevator, a couple of guys from finance were speaking in a code that Holly understood — cuts.

They were coming, and Holly could see them cresting the horizon like soldiers in a battle line. He had no weapon against them. No one did. Cuts were part of the business cycle, a pattern that had developed over time and was indicative of poor management, not market forces. He loathed cuts.

Holly knew things weren't going well. *It's all in the numbers.* He was a numbers man in a people area; while others looked at more qualitative metrics and considered human figures, he homed in on the quantitative kind. They never lied.

But he did. It really wasn't lying, he thought, it was being selective about the truth. He had said to Sloane many times that quantifying HR was a challenge. KPIs, cost-benefit analysis,

ROI — those were finance terms. You can't draw a straight line to productivity, he asserted. You can't measure people with the same metrics you use for products. She agreed but insisted that he find a way. It's imperative that we demonstrate our direct contribution to the bottom line, she'd said. That was code for wanting recognition, for her group's work to be seen as value adding. HR was viewed as operational, and it was. But Sloane felt her team was a strategic asset to the company, transforming leaders, galvanizing teams, inspiring individuals. Her enthusiasm was infectious, and Holly found himself feeling energized on more than one occasion. It was why he liked working for her. She was drawn to possibilities, and she often made the right moves — for the company and for herself. Holly understood that outshining her peers was important as a validation for her team, but more so for herself. He did what he could to support her.

His fibs were minor. He might combine data from a couple of the teams in order to mask a harmless deviation that might otherwise raise questions. Or he might provide a net number for new hires and turnover to blur the number of people actually leaving. Harmless fabrications.

Regardless, it all made Holly's stomach hurt, and he ate antacids as if they were mints.

His only desire was to get out on the golf course, pull out a club, exert force, and lash at the horizon. He had a few more years. He and his wife had found an ideal twenty-five-acre parcel with its own lake, three heritage cabins, and a chicken coop. It was midway between their children's homes and a mere thirty minutes away from two golf courses. Jack Nicklaus had played at one of them.

Whatever was in the notebook was personal and important to Sloane, and clearly it was something of value to someone else, because it hadn't yet turned up. *Where was Poirot at a time like this?* All the suspects had been together at the morning meeting.

He chuckled at the thought that it was a team meeting. There was nothing team about the group. You're supposed to compete against others, on the outside, he thought, they were busy stepping over each other. It was Darwinian. *Can't trust anybody.* That added to the stress. He reached for another antacid.

He didn't spend a lot of time thinking about his colleagues, but a moment like this caused him to pause and rehash some judgments: Vivian is the most peculiar, he thought. So many attention seekers on this team, but she is the worst. She's everywhere, all the time. She turns up to every meeting, responds to every chat or email or text. She's always speaking but really doesn't have much to say other than to tell everyone how much she worked and how understaffed she was. She seemed to be strapped for everything but time. He didn't understand people like that. Clearly, he thought, this is an effect from childhood. But good grief, she's an adult and this is a place of business. I wish I could ignore her like Baptiste does.

Holly thought Baptiste wasn't much better. He reeked of Uriah Heep. The only thing missing was the hand wringing. They steered clear of each other. Holly presumed that Baptiste was cagey and guarded because he knew that Holly could see through him like glass. Holly was surprised how many people Baptiste had influenced into believing that he held some specialized knowledge about people and organizations. So many of them say he's wise, thought Holly. I think he's full of shit. A real puffer.

Holly liked Charlotte but was skeptical about Alys and Jack, and hadn't landed a definitive opinion about Dimitri. Sloane had favorites, and Alys and Jack were them. Both stank of insecurity, but that comes in many flavors, thought Holly, and they each had their own tang. On the surface he liked Dimitri. The guy knows his stuff. He can quote chapter and verse on company policy. He's practically an encyclopedia. Holly had never met anyone who studied corporate guidelines and processes the way Dimitri did. There was something about that though that just didn't seem right.

Yes, what would Poirot do? Well, it didn't matter. The notebook was here in front of him. Holly paused to think about what he was going to do. He had no interest in looking inside. It was private. He could take it to Sloane, he thought. Nah, that would mean a load of questions. He could hand it off to Amelia. Nah, he thought, same issue. I'll just leave it. Someone else will come along and find it. Likely it will be Amelia anyway. The glasses and cups were stockpiling in the sink. She came by with regularity to ensure everything was tidy. No doubt she'd be here soon.

ALYS

On Friday afternoon, following the close of the offsite, Alys arrived home exhausted. As she approached the front door, she heard her husband's muffled voice and her boys playing and laughing. She paused. Suddenly Alys imagined her boys as men, and her mind drifted to Baptiste.

It was just last month that she'd decided she would take him as her lover. She had grown restless at home and couldn't quite put her finger on what she needed. After eighteen years with William, there was no subject left to discuss, no film or novel to analyze, no gossip to share, no desire of any kind to express. Nothing. They looked at one another but didn't see each other. Her world was quiet, and she was uneasy and exhausted.

Alys loved her boys, and she also loved William. But. There was always a but. She'd read several books about how to rekindle their romance: spend quality time together, listen attentively, go on dates, express feelings and needs, acknowledge and celebrate each other. The books even suggested prioritizing physical intimacy. *Yeah easy, just wedge that in between after school pick up and dinner. Blah, blah, blah.* What she needed wasn't to be found on the best-seller list.

She needed spark. She needed fire. What she wanted was to light the flame elsewhere and then carry it home to light William's cauldron of desire. So, after much consideration, she embroidered a story about how to save her marriage. And it involved Baptiste.

He was safe. No one, she thought, *no one* would ever suspect that they would hook up. And he wasn't someone she could fall in love with. Had she sought out a stranger, it could happen. With Baptiste, she knew emphatically it would not. He struck her as a man who liked men and women. In fact, she knew he did but couldn't put her finger on how she knew it. Everyone assumed he was gay, even though he never shared a single word about his personal life. But she felt it. She had considered every detail, played out a multitude of scenarios, and surveyed him several times. He had fine muscle tone and big hands. His butt was tight, his hips narrow, and his mind sharp. Nothing more was needed.

He was a classic manipulator. His vulnerabilities textbook. She would pull his strings, plant the seeds of desire, and allow him to feel as if he was the hunter. He was a man after all.

Alys had been right. Over the course of the offsite, she sat next to him, found ways to pair up, laughed a lot, touched his arm, flattered him. The first night in the bar, she positioned herself across from him so that they would continuously make eye contact and speak to each other. One by one, their colleagues went up to their respective rooms. The only one left was Amelia, who was lingering at the bar. Alys guessed that she, too, had identified prey.

Alys felt carefree. The drinks certainly helped. Baptiste was both predictable and at the same time lacked a pattern. He asked about family, childhood, university. At one point he challenged her feminism. She thought the conversation might lead to heightened sexual tension, but it didn't. At least not at that moment. They talked about work, colleagues, Sloane. Alys gave away light gossip but held back anything of real value. She even made a few things up. She was fond of Sloane, she said, and offered opinions on all her colleagues. Those were truthful. Too many lies would be hard to juggle.

She was not nervous. She couldn't say why, but she wasn't. When they got to her room, he immediately took command. His skill as a lover was to her advantage. He undressed her, caressed her, and explored her body. He set her on fire — exactly as planned. He came to her room every night thereafter.

Alys went into the supply room around two o'clock. She needed markers and post-its. She had a client meeting — part of her side hustle — and she was gathering supplies. As she was looking on a lower shelf, she spotted the notebook. She opened it to a page with a list of conferences, locations, and hotels. She flipped a few pages to a list of what appeared to be login names. No, user passwords. They were curious:

craftytiger   slowninja
loneeagle   hiddenfiddler

Strange. Perhaps she generated these out of some kind of app? Could be helpful, something to investigate.

"Hey, Alys"

She froze at Amelia's voice.

Alys closed the notebook and turned slowly. She casually held the notebook in her hand.

"How are you my dear? Find what you're looking for?"

"No" said Amelia. "I'm so puzzled by this."

"And Sloane?"

"So unhappy."

"Terrible way to start the week."

"It sure is."

"Well, I certainly hope you find it. Do let me know, and of course if there is anything I can do." Alys gathered her markers and post-its and walked out the door.

TYPING...

Sloane: What is happening?

Amelia: Still looking for it

Amelia: At a loss

Sloane: Find anything else?

Amelia: No

Amelia: But several people are acting weird.

Amelia: Ran into Alys. She's cheerful...

Amelia: different

Sloane: How?

Amelia: Can't place it

Amelia: Kind of satisfied or something

Amelia: Same with Jack

Sloane: Will be back up at 4:30

Sloane: Talk then

Dimitri

Dimitri found it in the file room at one o'clock. The page he opened contained a list of names, and he soon realized they were people who had been fired over the past year. He recognized a few and then discovered the pattern: they were all from R&D and manufacturing. He remembered one termination in particular, a mid-level operator who had emailed a significant number of documents to his personal email. It was a clear violation of company policy.

Companies need policies and guidelines, thought Dimitri, but not for the reasons most people think. It's not about promoting or ensuring desired behavior, it's because companies want to have ammunition against employees. Companies know that rules can be broken, but more often, they're simply worked around. Companies also anticipate that loopholes will be found, and when they are and the violations exposed, the company will determine if there was intended breach or debatable misuse. The true purpose of a policy is to aid in the termination process. Most companies are selective in using policy this way, but they all do it.

He was right to think that privacy and confidentiality were at risk when Amelia announced the notebook missing. Whoever came in contact with the notebook was, in some way, being non-compliant. Perhaps he could work it to his advantage.

Dimitri and his partner were accomplished executives in different industries. Their career trajectories were similar, and success had embraced them both around the same time. They each held an executive position, and a slight but silent level of competition existed as they continued their professional climb. David was charismatic, and his personality catapulted him to the top. For Dimitri, it was hard work. What started as a way to get to know the ins and outs of a company and how it worked became a way to move up, and then move out. He dazzled his bosses with his level of knowledge. He showed them how to use policy to support people decisions, and when the time came to match one of David's promotions, Dimitri violated a policy, negotiated a package, and moved on. As he began to plan each departure, he also began to search for another role. His scheme was usually well-timed, and his credentials impressive. Finding a job had never been an issue. His parting agreement always ensured confidentiality, and to David he passed off his severance package as a sign-on bonus. Because they were in different industries, their paths and contacts never crossed professionally, and David was unaware.

Dimitri was discovered with another boy at the age of 15. His father, incredulous, stood stunned in the doorway of his bedroom. Time stopped. After that moment, his father wanted distance in all its forms. He turned, walked away, and refused to speak to his son. His mother cried and thereafter wore the colors of mourning. He was sent away to finish school and never returned to his family home.

Dimitri struggled with the inconsistency of his feelings: shame for letting his parents down, and exhilaration at the discovery of who he really was. The pain of his parent's rejection left a wake of anxiety that he could not shake and one that he carried into his relationships. Without a partner, he was alone in the world. Another aspect of himself that was new and unconventional.

He met David one afternoon at the dry cleaner while waiting in the rush hour line. They exchanged casual conversation, commented on the harsh fluorescent lighting, and noted how much business was conducted in such an inelegant operation. They always seemed to be waiting in line together, and after several such encounters, they adjourned to a nearby sports bar for a beer. They had been together ever since. David was alive with intelligence and ambition, and he was pleased that both he and Dimitri were successful in their careers. Dimitri was pleased too, but he quietly feared that one day he might not be able to match David in his ascent. Occasionally, his alarm manifested in his dreams, and he'd wake drenched with lingering questions: *What if one day I'm not enough? What if he also turns away?*

Dimitri was now hoping to be a casualty of cuts. David was nearing another major milestone, and Dimitri was preparing for his own move. The position changes didn't happen with frequency but pulling them off meant planning. The cuts could work in his favor. He could take the notebook to Sloane, feign concern, and return it with a vague story about how it came to be in his possession, give a hint about its content, but remain vague enough that Sloane would wonder. He knew her well enough to know that she would feel compromised. To know something private about her was to hold a card to be played against her. She would never risk it.

As he was mulling over his options and reviewing the list of names again, he decided not to take it to Sloane. He played out her chess moves, acknowledging her as the better player. She could strategically use this to her advantage, showcase it publicly in some favorable way, demonstrate her magnanimous leadership, declare how much she trusted her team, and then retaliate privately. She could make a show of thanking everyone for mobilizing to find her notebook with all its confidential information, she might praise him specifically as he was the one who brought it back to her, underscoring his understanding of policies that governed such matters, and under the guise of rewarding him she would find ways to bring him down for having crossed a line, because she couldn't know what he had seen.

If that were to happen, he thought, she would fight for no severance, and win. After all, he had taught her how to use the
policies.

No, he thought, I'll leave it where I found it.

Vivian

The ruckus had hardly died down when Vivian discovered the notebook in the copy room. It was eleven o'clock, and she didn't have a meeting for another two hours. She was still seething at Baptiste after the morning meeting. *That arrogant beast!* How could he sit across from someone and never make eye contact? Vivian had bored holes into his eyes, but he was as impassive as a boulder.

Vivian and Charlotte had discussed Baptiste's behavior on many occasions. He treated them both with disdain. They cared because you can't feel a sense of belonging when you are being shut out. It was so disrespectful.

Well okay, she thought, if he doesn't feel that Charlotte is on his same par, I understand. She's a kind and lovely woman, but there's nothing special about her — no unique talent, nothing overly engaging in her personality. Vivian acknowledged that everyone on the team had some talent, but she knew she was the star.

Oh sure, Jack vied for Sloane's attention. You might as well rename Jack to Joe because he was so average. Nothing spectacular other than his flattery. And Ralph Hollingsworth III. He was parked and waiting. Holly would do nothing to lose his place. He only had a few more years before golf and grandkids took over his life. And Alys. Mrs. Extreme Extrovert, Vivian thought. She talks all the time, just like a spoiled child, and her voice ticks along like a metronome. It's so very irritating. Dimitri is the opposite: quiet, inward, suspicious.

And then there's Amelia. Vivian liked her. A hard worker, staying late copying and filing. Vivian knew this because she also worked late every night. There was too much to do, and she didn't have enough staff. Sloane wouldn't provide her with more people resources and wouldn't allocate more funds for raises either. Vivian found a small concession by giving out accolades and spot bonuses. Her people were always appreciative, and they showered her with praise. Vivian wanted a raise, she wanted a promotion, and she wanted more money for her team, and she was working hard to convince Sloane that it was required.

Vivian grew up in a home defined by scarcity. Her mother's constant complaints about being penniless painted their world with the absence of hope. Her family rarely had enough food to go around — some days, they passed a can of beans so each could take turns with a spoon. But Vivian was never paralyzed by poverty. Instead, it fueled her. She dedicated herself to her studies and engaged in extracurricular activities, reaching for the rungs of the ladder that would lift her out of the hellacious pit into which she had been born. Her efforts generated significant profits: scholarships were awarded, internships granted, and career opportunities unfolded. Indeed, she worked her way out, up, and into the executive ranks.

Vivian took nothing for granted though. She continued to exhaust herself with work, performing tasks that she should have delegated long ago. She felt it imperative that her colleagues know her level of dedication, the many hours of her toil, and the sacrifices she was making. While she didn't fear poverty, neither could she savor success.

Vivian took a deep breath and opened the notebook. At first, she couldn't make out what she was looking at. It appeared to be a list. Of people. How they were connected. How they were recruited to the company, or who by. Mentors identified. It was like reading the Bible.

> Joseph Wilson brought Mei Chen and
> Aisha Khan
> *Mei Chen mentored Jamal Washing-
> ton who recruited Carlos Silva

And on it went. Ten dense pages of names and relationships. Next to each name, there was either an X or a Y, mostly Ys. Vivian was confused. But that's why Sloane was the boss, she thought, she looks at things through various lenses. Clearly this list had yielded some benefit, but for what — or who — Vivian could not be sure. She flipped around a few more pages, still perplexed, and closed the notebook. It wasn't a big deal after all. She decided to leave it on the trail for Amelia to find and headed for the file room.

Lost and Found

Amelia spied it from twenty feet away. She quickly whisked it off the corner of her desk and opened it. Relief flooded her. *Thank God.* What a day it had been, but now the ordeal was over.

THE RETURN

Sloane appeared like lightning. As soon as she saw the smile on Amelia's face, she felt the tension drain away. Amelia raised the notebook and handed it back to Sloane.

"Someone left it on my desk." Amelia said. "I don't know who."

Sloane was silent. She began to pace.

"Something sneaky is going on here," Sloane said. "You texted that people were acting funny. Who?"

"All of them. Everyone I came across. Lots of hushed voices and quick exits."

Sloane stopped pacing and looked out at the snow for a moment, her back to Amelia. "Well, I can't thank you enough for helping to get it back. I know it's taken you off schedule for the day, and it's been stressful and tiring. What a mishap! But here it is." Sloane patted it with her right hand.

"I'll have to look through it to see if there is anything unkind or disturbing that someone might have read," said Sloane. "And I will find out who." Her sneer turned into a smile that she beamed at Amelia. "Thank you again."

Sloane had more meetings at the top of the hour. Amelia was going to make one last round through the copy and conference rooms, check the kitchen, and then go home.

PEN TO PAPER

It was after seven o'clock when Sloane sat down at her desk and opened her notebook. She flipped the pages. *Who was it? And what did they see?* She began to write:

> I've been tense all day, worrying
> about who might find this and what
> they might read. My private thoughts.
> My private notes. Someone found it
> and intentionally kept it all day. All
> day! Did they read it from cover to
> cover? If so, I'll deny anything
> anyone says.

She raised the Bic pen to her mouth.

> I couldn't help but think of Harriet
> throughout the day. This happened to
> her too. And she came out of it a
> winner. I will too. Spies rarely get
> caught.

Her thoughts flowed: Amelia had found some copied scraps of information. They were, indeed, from her notebook. Why would anyone want that? It was information unrelated to anyone on the team. She had replayed the morning meeting in her head so many times, and still couldn't pinpoint the moment when the notebook was taken. Amelia had been seated on one side, and Charlotte on the other.

"Think, Sloane!" She said out loud. What happened? But she couldn't find anything in her memory and so immediately turned her attention to a retribution strategy. And also, a mitigation strategy. What if Jack had found out that he wasn't getting the promotion? What if Baptiste had discovered he was going to be cut? Dimitri might have seen that he would be asked to take over Baptiste's function until the organization could be redesigned. The others might have viewed their performance feedback. Her eyes widened. *Argh!*

The notebook contained a lot more than just that, but she knew each individual well enough to know what would be important to them. Mostly, she thought, it contains my personal opinions and experiences. *They're real and they're mine, and they're not for dispute.* From early in her career, Sloane was told repeatedly to keep her professional life and personal life separate. And I do that, she thought. I don't socialize with co-workers, definitely not with direct reports, and I only lightly share anecdotes of family activities. Just enough, nothing too personal. But my notebook represents my life: it's professional, and it's personal. I make no distinctions. And it is no one's business. What I think and what I write in my notebook are private. If you come across it, you're the one in the wrong. Period.

The day had felt like a Frida Kahlo painting; her raw internality exposed, and now Sloane wanted Mark Rothko's soothing color fields. And a glass of wine.

Exhausted, she began to gather her belongings. The snow continued to fall outside the window. It's rhythm had mirrored the events of the day: sometimes slow and lethargic, sometimes fast and vigorous.

Amelia

I couldn't afford to be found out. When I realized my notebook was missing, I panicked. It's never happened before.

Like Shakespeare said:

All the world's a stage
And all the men and women merely players
They have their exits and their entrances
And one man in his time plays many parts

I certainly have.

The first part was easy – easy to get and easy to perform.

I joined almost six months ago with a general assignment to gather as much information as possible. R&D and manufacturing are always of highest interest, but there is much to steal from a company this size. Such as identifying current or former employees who might turn and provide information, or sourcing people who were terminated that might want revenge — that's why I'm in HR, for the access to personnel data — it's my specialty.

I amplified my role of keeping common areas neat and free of confidential information. It gave me a legitimate reason to conduct sweeps, to look at the copy machine and in the trash bins. If someone saw me, my behavior wouldn't be questioned: it's part of the job. I take any and every opportunity I can to uncover information.

No one ever suspects the admin. Not at this level anyway. They are friendly and respectful, but they're always superior. No one thinks an admin knows anything. We're too busy putting away the dirty dishes that they're too lazy to load or tucking chairs back under the conference table or disposing of bottles of free soda and water.

What they don't consider is that admins are given access – access to their manager's calendar and their manager's email and their manager's files. Other leaders who can't seem to schedule a meeting on their own also open their calendars, and sometimes open access to their email too. Some do it for status. Others for efficiency. It's a real treasure trove.

The higher in an organization you go as an admin, the more information you access. Executive admins are a strong network. We hold confidences greater than anyone else in the company, and we share things among ourselves that no one else knows. It's a perfect network for a spy.

Our managers are too saturated with pomposity and don't really have time to think about us as anything other than a pair of hands.

"Amelia, could you get me a coke please?"

I've been meticulous in my cataloguing. I've passed along lists of consultants, meeting planners, and anyone connected to leadership events. The same for key leaders and employees in critical roles. All get surveilled: homes monitored, trash picked over, wireless networks penetrated. At conferences and meetings, we keep eyes on their hotel rooms, enter and rifle through their belongings, and access any technology that is not secure in the hotel safe. We place operatives in the bars, looking for people enjoying a bit of play away from their spouses, and if we have intel or inclination that says they'll fall for a honey trap, we set it. That's why I keep track of dates, conferences, locations, hotels, and the like.

It was my notebook that went missing, not Sloane's. I needed a diversion so that I could find and retrieve it, and I needed a cover story. So, I took hers. No one was the wiser. I don't know who picked my notebook up, and if or how it was passed around, though I do think it was. I'm fairly certain they don't know what they saw. They were trying to align the content with Sloane and their expectations of her. What they were actually reading was a biography of deception.

As part of my onboarding, I was provided with an org chart of Sloane's direct reports — a visual depicting the team. But this group is not a team, and the lines didn't accurately show the relationships. Quite a few links were missing, as loyalties and allegiances aren't based on hierarchy. That's why I drew them as a planetary system, always moving and rotating.

When I texted Sloane, I'd pulled items from her notebook that I knew were innocuous, but sensitive enough to give rise to a bit of panic on her part. And I blew on those embers.

Sloane's notebook has never been of much interest to me.

After the many times I interrupted her writing in it, I realized that she was just scribbling thoughts. There was very little desirable company information, particularly anything of confidential value. Sloane has a solid memory and a keen sense for what not to put down on paper. She also has an acerbic tongue that translates to the page. I cringed at some of the things she wrote about people. And yet she has genuine concern, too, and can be rather complimentary. She's a paradox. Definitely hard to square.

I should clearly state that, on the one hand, I like Sloane. She's not a bad person — she's a wounded person. Aren't we all? She is demanding and duplicitous, yet kind and generous. And she's smart and courageous and has achieved her success primarily through her own efforts, her own energy, her own intellect. I've witnessed her berate Baptiste, lie to Jack, and dismiss Charlotte. She can be a true Basilisk, and her storms are nasty. I hate every aspect of this, but I don't hate her. In fact, I'm rather fond of her. We share a love of literature, and we work and think well together. I mean, she loves Antonio Tabucchi. How many people even know his novels?

In my experience — ha! Picked that up from Sloane — people either play to win or play not to lose. I'm on Sloane's side and think crushing it should be everyone's goal.

To me, the Vivians of the world are the most tragic. So many evenings when I was copying documents and inspecting files, Vivian was in her office working until late. No matter what she said about it, no one cared. I don't think she's defined by the poverty of her youth, but it is a significant part of her identity. No matter how much she tries to deny or suppress it, which she tries to do, she should honor it for the gift it provided: a noble determination over defeat. She does deserve recognition, but not for the reasons she espouses. Unfortunately, she'll always be in the throes of the struggle, unable to revel in the joys of success.

I blanched at a lot of what I observed — so much inappropriate conduct. Baptiste and Alys share scars from youth and are cut from the same cloth, though they each approach the game differently. I must give Baptiste some credit though. He's well-liked as a leader because he's great at explaining *the why* – which is what people always want to know — and he works with people to uncover their potential and drive them toward their passions, to be authentically who they are without shame. I suspect he knows a thing or two about that. But that doesn't excuse his arrogant behavior and the shameful way he treats some people.

I enjoyed working with them. All of them. At one point, I foolishly thought I might defect. A fleeting thought because what I've learned about organizations is that the focus is always on repairing the symptoms instead of addressing the root cause. Behavior is often influenced by the structure — what you see on the chart — and the reward systems which, frankly, incentivize the wrong outcome.

You're probably wondering how I could do this and what's in it for me. Well, it's a job. I studied literature and, as Pessoa

said, "Literature is the most agreeable way of ignoring life [...]
it is the most concrete of all things because it is the most real."
But that reality doesn't translate into a profession or a job nec-
essarily. Like Sloane, I had dreams of being a writer. After I grad-
uated, I found a job with a consulting company writing
narratives based on competitive analysis. I was good at it —
taking data and crafting compelling stories, transforming information into something engaging, and they liked me. So they
opened up and invited me into intelligence gathering, which
is how I got here.

Do I harbor any guilt for what I am doing? Not really. I do
understand that it's wrong; I also know stealing secrets is illegal.
But companies conduct this type of intelligence in a variety of
ways — some above the law, some below. Aside from a lot of
data analytics on public information, companies typically
poach talent and with them comes information.

Pessoa also said that everything we see is something else.
So am I.

What about you?

Epilogue

Holly sat at his desk. It had been a long day — tense as a result of Sloane's missing notebook — and he had thought about Poirot more and more the longer the mystery remained. Holly closed his eyes and conjured his favorite French detective:

They were nine around the long white table. Poirot rose to speak, and the variegated chatter tapered into silence.

Messieurs et Mesdames, we are here because of the matter of the missing notebook. You all know the facts of the case. At 9 o'clock this morning, the nine of you met in this conference room for your weekly staff meeting. Each with a notebook, laptop, phone or some combination. All provided by the company. And, as you know, all similar in appearance. During the course of the meeting, you sat here, as you are now, conducting your business, and at some point stood and shifted to stand in front of the flip chart in the corner. At 10 o'clock, with great punctuality, Madame Sloane adjourned the session, and you gathered your belongings and departed.

It was at this time the notebook was found to be missing. We are therefore forced to conclude that the notebook was taken by someone in this room. Was it by accident? Or was it premeditated? Perhaps it was something different altogether? I have a theory that I will put forward to you.

"It's just a notebook," Jack interrupted.

Now ladies and gentlemen, I must tell you that it was not just a notebook. It was the notebook of one of the company's *senior* executives. A repository of sensitive organizational information, private thoughts, and perhaps other items of which we cannot fathom.

Everyone shifted slightly in their seats.

"And how is that different than mine, or any other notebook? Why didn't someone take mine then?"

You have asked a very good question, Madame Alys. I thought of it myself. When I heard all the evidence, of which there is very little, I had to think about the *why*, and what came to my mind was that there were certain points, like the one you have just made, that were worthy of greater attention.

What are these possibilities? Let me share them now. As I mentioned already, your notebooks and resources are all company issue, with the same design. What's more, all of you, with a few exceptions which I will touch on momentarily, have access to the same information. Same databases. Same employee information. Same financial information. Only two of you hold variations. That is you, Madame Sloane, and you, Mademoiselle Amelia.

So I had to think. *Why?* Why would someone take the notebook of Madame Sloane? What would they be looking for? What might they find?

I had to consider Monsieur Jack. Always first to speak up, as you witnessed earlier. He is a loyal man, polite, content to live in the shadow of his wife's success. And also that of Madame Sloane. He is personable, and yet he offers very little of himself. A man like this wishes to be carried forward by others. He lacks true ambition and yet proudly steps into the spotlight when someone leaves it for another stage. A man such as this, however, is not harmless. This passivity can be detrimental. For when the ladder he climbs becomes unstable, or the hand that pulls him upward hesitates, he will move with vigor and those actions will be out of desperation.

Monsieur Jack is a stark contrast to Monsieur Baptiste. What a presence! What a performer! Meticulously dressed, the picture of precision, a man who likes his world ordered, revealing a vanity and a need for control. He is seen as a man of action. He is seen as a man of wisdom. A tilt of the head, a British accent, a thoughtful pause, and *voilà!* He has convinced you that he is a man of profound insight. But is he? *Non, mes amis.* Monsieur Baptiste is not wise; he is clever. A man of the theatre; he is a manipulator. He is not evil, but he is not genuine; and when a man is not genuine, he is dangerous. He plays his part so convincingly that even he forgets it is a role. But the truth, it always waits in the wings, does it not?

And I also had to examine Madame Alys. She smiles and speaks with practiced ease. She laughs, loudly, and one wonders what her laughter hides. She tells stories, always about others, never about herself, and yet she enjoys the attention, craves a listener. But beneath the charm, there is a hard edge — a disappointment, one that suggest she is not as lighthearted as she seems. There is a bitterness, an aftertaste left by childhood. She feels that men are and have always been the privileged ones. That they have it all: the attention, the respect, the power. And in this, she is partly right perhaps. But she does not see that her own actions, her own condemnations, have not elevated her or other women. Her voice so loud and her denunciations so one-sided, that she has lost all credibility.

And I was puzzled by Madame Vivian. She is a most industrious woman, *non*? She works long hours, always reminding us – subtly, of course – of her sacrifices. She sees herself as the one who holds it all together. And yet, her ambition, it is not entirely selfless. *Non*, not at all. She speaks of her department, her team, her goals, but beneath it all lies the truth: she wishes to rise, and she believes she deserves to. She has overcome much in her life through sheer will and an unclouded perspective. Yet she cannot see her own flaws, and when one lacks objectivity, they don't always make sound decisions.

Then we have Madame Charlotte, a woman with clarity of purpose. She is committed, *oui*, to her family and her goals, and she will withstand anything to ensure they are well and secure. She mumbles her mantras and meditations to keep herself in balance, to maintain a sense of peace, but these practices — they are not merely for relaxation, no. They are her shield. They are her fortress. But pressure can crack impenetrable walls, and the peaceful inner focus can shift to the outer world. And then what can happen?

Ah, Monsieur Holly. A man who has spent his life on the wheel of incessant toil, always reliable, always respectable. He has achieved much — his position is high, his reputation untarnished — but now, he dreams only of the quiet life. Rounds of golf and the laughter of grandchildren. These are the luxuries he has worked to earn. And yet, while he can see the horizon of retirement, the stresses and the office politics continue to bring him pain – or heartburn to be more precise. He is a man who is already halfway out the door. And a man like that, *mes amis*, will do almost anything to keep his path to the exit clear.

So unlike Monsieur Dimitri, who has a plan and a timeline. He is a man of policies and fine print who understands the nuances that lead to manipulation. He knows exactly where and how circumstances can work to his advantage, or against that of others. He is polite and charming and will guide you and suggest to you, and then one day, he will walk you to the door, smile, and say, "It's policy." Beware, *non*?

And you, Mademoiselle Amelia, you discovered all of this did you not? The ideal assistant, the one who sees all, hears all, and makes note of everything. She sits at her desk, quietly typing, answering calls, arranging meetings. A simple role, one might think. But *non*, she is clever. So clever that she believes the rest of us are amateurs at the game of deception.

And so *mes amis*, we see it clearly: each one of you could stand to gain from taking Madame Sloane's notebook, yet only one of you did. But why?

It's not the reason that you may believe.

Is it, Mademoiselle?

Acknowledgments

Deep gratitude to Tom — for all the years, all the love, all the support, and all the laughter. Thanks for listening to the stories.

Big, huge thanks to Jayne Marshall for her friendship, support, superb editorial contributions which have made this story better in so many ways, and for a great partnership in helping to build Modern Odyssey Books.

As always, enormous thanks to Claire Wirdnam for reading and providing thoughtful commentary and for unwavering support and deep friendship.

And to David Bloch and Sajni Patel for assisting with business matters and important story details, and also for providing overall feedback. Much appreciated.

About the Author

Maria Glymph is a writer and the publisher of Modern Odyssey Books.

Prior publications by Maria include *Barn Quilt: Poems* and *Hope, Time, and Other Things That Are Hard to Measure*. She is also the creative imagination behind the *In Search Of* series of literature-inspired puzzle books (Charles Dickens, Jane Austen, the Brontë Sisters, Shakespeare, Homer, and more to come).

As the founder and publisher of Modern Odyssey Books, she is expanding the imprint's list to include an array of global authors writing poetry, literary fiction, creative non-fiction, and other narrative forms.

Maria splits her time between her writing pursuits and building Modern Odyssey Books as a respected independent publisher.

Keep up with her at www.mariaglymph.com.

Extra Ink

And why not consider Madame Sloane? It was her notebook that was taken, was it not? And she is formidable, *non*? A woman at the top of her field, commanding respect, wielding authority, moving with confidence, speaking with precision. She is clever, yes, but also ruthless. Loyalty? It is a word for others. Truth? She twists it, bends it, until it fits her purpose. She does not mean to harm — no, in her heart, she believes she is doing what is necessary, what is deserved. But she cannot see her own behavior, how it leaves others crushed in its wake. Such a woman, *mes amis*, is dangerous not because she is cruel, but because she believes her actions are justified. She lies with charm, betrays with ease, all in pursuit of the prize. And yet, in her heart, there is still a flicker of goodness — a part of her that wishes for connection, for kindness, though she buries it beneath her ambition. So, we must ask: what did she do with her notebook?

References

(in order of appearance)

1. *Harriet the Spy* by Louise Fitzhugh
2. The Hatter, *Alice's Adventures in Wonderland* by Lewis Carroll
3. Maryse Condé
4. Nikos Kazantzakis
5. Albert Camus
6. Franz Kafka
7. Jane Austen
8. Kate Chopin
9. The Five Dysfunctions of a Team *by Patrick Lencioni*
11. *The Fifth Discipline* by Peter Senge
12. *Reinventing Organizations* by Frederic Laloux
13. Peter Block
14. Edgar Schein
15. Jay Galbraith
16. *Die Brücke*, German Expressionist art group
17. *Stargirl* by Jerry Spinelli
18. *The Thinker*, Auguste Rodin
19. *Girl Before a Mirror*, Pablo Picasso
20. *Each Kindness* by Jacqueline Woodson
21. *The Gulf Stream* by Winslow Homer
22. *A Sunday Afternoon on the Island of La Grande Jatte* by Georges Seurat
23. *Hour of the Star* by Clarice Lispector
24. "Better a thousand enemies outside the house than one inside,"
    — Arabic proverb
25. "When you first rise in the morning tell yourself: I will encounter busybodies,
    ingrates, egomaniacs, liars, the jealous and cranks." — Marcus Aurelius
26. Hercule Poirot, Agatha Christie's fictional Belgian detective
27. *Table of Nations*, a genealogical listing in the Book of Genesis in the Bible
28. Frida Kahlo
29. Mark Rothko
30. "All the world's a stage..." — *As You Like It*, William Shakespeare
31. "Literature is the most agreeable way of ignoring life." — Fernando Pessoa
32. "Everything we see is something else" (a paraphrase of "What we see isn't
    what we see, but what we are.") — Fernando Pessoa

About Modern Odyssey Books

Modern Odyssey Books publishes literary fiction, poetry, creative nonfiction, short story collections, and other narrative forms. In addition, Modern Odyssey produces the literature-inspired *In Search of...* puzzle book series.

www.modernodysseybooks.com

Our Titles

Poetry, Literary Fiction, Essays
Barn Quilt: Poems
Hope, Time, and Other Things That Are Hard to Measure
A Line Drawn or Printed: Six Routes Through Madrid

In Search of...
(our literature-inspired puzzle books)
Charles Dickens
Jane Austen
The Brontë Sisters
Shakespeare
Homer

ISBN: 979-8-9900395-9-9

Modern Odyssey Books
Maria Glymph, Publisher
www.modernodysseybooks.com